Vive l'Empereur

" The throne of France is no longer held in my hand or in yours."

Vive l'Empereur

By

Mary Raymond Shipman Andrews

Illustrated by F. C. Yohn

Charles Scribner's Sons
New York . . . 1902

UNIVERSITY PRESS, JOHN WILSON
AND SON · CAMBRIDGE, U. S. A.

TO HER MEMORY FOR
WHOM IT WAS WRITTEN

Illustrations

From drawings by F. C. Yohn

Vive l'Empereur

Chapter One

ONLY a Frenchwoman could have been so charming a hostess as was the Baroness to her unknown guests. And it was a difficult business. The tall, fair-haired youngest of them, who spoke his fluent French a bit stiffly, alone seconded her gracious efforts to make friends of these four strangers. The old officer was kindly but shy, and, moreover, nervous. As for the two who had come in together, they were frankly preoccupied. Their eyes were on the door, and responsive as they evidently wished to be, the quality of their responsiveness was strained. But the lad, though the color came and went in his fresh face, and though he started, like the others, at a sound from outside, yet listened to her, talked to her, with the manner she was used to — as if there were no other person on earth. More than that, he came to her aid at every turn with a breezy enthusiasm and a great, hearty laugh, to help her trap the others in her friendly net. The Baroness, out of a full experience, gave him a long good mark for blood and breeding. Her amused eye swept the four of them.

"Pooh! A good old bear, and two nervous greyhounds! But the

boy — it is a born war-horse! He feels the thunder in the air and thrills, yet stands steady. The Prince will see quickly enough what stuff he has here." And at the thought, the door opened, and, unannounced, the Prince came in.

Wherever that limping figure stood was the centre of the room, and in a second they were grouped about him. While he bowed low over the Baroness's eager little hand, the clear, light eyes had already seen each of the others. It was easy for the most accomplished performer on the human instrument in Europe to mix deftly this oil and water where even the charm of the Baroness had failed. A fleeting smile embraced the two anxious conspirators, and the shiver-

3

ing cockles of their hearts warmed, and at once they knew that they were great and wise men and masters of craft, even as he. A glance of such earnest, whole-souled honesty met the look of Marshal Victor that the old soldier felt with relief that the sincerity and devotion which he had begun to fear extinct were personified here. Then the blue eyes turned their calm, assured look on the lad in the background, and the two gazed for a moment at each other on a level, for this lame old man was tall and broad-shouldered, too. The fine, keen face, with its lines of power and lines of misanthropy, its look of race that was, perhaps, more striking than either, brightened to gracious friendliness.

4

Not the least of the gifts of Charles
Maurice de Talleyrand-Périgord was
a vein of genuineness that ran through
the carefully laid artificial strata of
his soul. The eager face pleased
him, and it might be convenient to
control the warm heart shining so
close behind it. At all events, it
was simple enough for Talleyrand,
so ———

"Ah! We have the young marshal! The little Michael! My lad,
the last time I saw you, you sat on my
knee. I thank you not to do it now.
Mon Dieu, no! You are a giant, a
Western giant! Has the Princess
of Moskowa seen you, then? Were
you to her taste? Did she not find
you strong and handsome?" The
blushing, laughing youngster was

given no time to answer. "Madame the Baroness," the Prince went on, "you must know that my great little Michael here is from foreign parts, from the wonderful America, where I have been also — they loved me very much, those good Americans. *Mon Dieu!* It was droll how the citizens of Philadelphia loved me! But that is aside. My Michael has lived with his father, the great —— "

Talleyrand stopped and looked at his audience.

"What, is it possible you do not know who the boy's father is!" He gazed around with astonishment; at good Marshal Victor, a little dazed; at the other men pulling their mustaches and looking bored; at the Baroness, flushed and interested.

6

"Look, then, all of you, at his face." A vivid red shot up to the boy's eyes and he found the situation embarrassing. "You do not see it, the resemblance? And yet it is striking. There is one in the house, then, who will see it. Madame, will you permit me to ring for my man?" He pulled the handle of a long cord that swung from the ceiling, and the door opened at once.

"You will send the servant of M. le Prince," the Baroness said. A gray-headed, soldierly looking man, in the Périgord livery, appeared.

"François," said the Prince, "you remember, perhaps, an execution behind the Luxembourg — I believe you were one of the detail — on a December morning in the year 1815?"

The man opened startled eyes and answered, stammering: "But, yes, Monseigneur."

"Then look at that young man and tell me who he is."

The scared face of the servant turned with the Prince's gaze to Michael, who was growing more and more uncomfortable. As his eyes rested on Michael's face, all his respect for so distinguished a company could not control an exclamation: "*Mon Dieu! Mon Dieu!*" he said. "*C'est lui — c'est lui-même!*"

The Prince waited a moment to let the dramatic force of the situation take a firm hold of the startled circle.

"Ah!" he said, smiling a satisfied smile, "I see you have not forgotten, then, François, that the Bourbons

8

forced you to shoot — to shoot *at* — your old commander, your adored general, the 'bravest of the brave.' Good, François. Perhaps you may yet strike a blow under his son. You may go, François." The man, his eyes lingering, clinging to Michael's face, slowly left the room. " I think you know now whom we have here," said Talleyrand, laying a cordial hand on Michael's shoulder.

Then as the two old officers of Napoleon, the truth dawning on them, turned excitedly toward the son of their comrade, the Prince's slender, strong fingers flew out in a quick gesture of command. "No! No heroics at this moment. He is, indeed, the son of Michael Ney — himself Michael Ney, and you may

9

take him and spoil him, if you can,
after this evening. But just now
there is an affair of moment before
us all. And in the meantime —
Madame, how careless I am! These
gentlemen," with a stately bow,
" await the honor of a presentation.
Permit me," with a deeper bending
toward the Baroness, " to present to
you your guests unknown, whom you
have had the amiability to receive for
me, my house being " — he flashed
a smile at them — " too highly ven-
tilated, shall we say? for social func-
tions of this sort. Madame the
Baroness, I have the honor to present
to you M. le Maréchal Victor, once
a point of light in Napoleon's star ;
himself to be a guiding star, soon, to
Napoleon's child." The grizzled old

warrior's eyes glowed as he made his bow. " And M. le Général Bertrand, who stood by Bonaparte's death-bed, but who will efface that sad memory presently when he stands by a new Bonaparte's throne. And M. Charles Teste, who is — but you know his name. Not head and front, perhaps, but backbone and hands he is of the great conspiracy that will soon place on the throne of France a strong race, fresh blood, a great name, the idol of the people — Napoleon's child."

"The King of Rome!" exclaimed Bertrand, a thrill of emotion in his voice.

Talleyrand turned on him a quick, queer look, quizzical, tolerant, knowing, masterful. "Napoleon's child," he repeated. " M. Teste, you, the hand on the pulse," a veiled note of sarcasm in his voice, " how is the plot going ? It grows like a mushroom, does it not ? What news have we ? "

From Teste's sharp, restless, dark eyes shot a hardly perceptible glance of hesitation toward the Baroness. Slight as it was the Prince caught it.

" We await you, Monsieur."

Teste, whose ancestors had not been, like Talleyrand's, great princes in the thirteenth century, was embarrassed. " Is it as well, Monsieur, to tell state secrets to an outsider — to a lady ? "

Talleyrand turned his head toward the small man with the impertinent grace that had made him the terror and the admiration of many another salon.

" *Mon ami,* aside from the fact that Madame the Baroness already knows the whole affair ; aside from the fact that, in her short day, she has known more affairs than you or most men ever heard of ; aside from all this, I grieve to see you lack that confidence in a woman which a good Frenchman should possess — I correct myself — should appear to possess. Is it possible that you lack also that confidence in me which you should possess — should appear to possess ? At this time I believe I have the honor to be necessary to your party. I also believe that I have before this — once or twice — been part of an arrangement, shall we call it ? con-

13

cerning thrones." Then the light
eyes narrowed to half their width,
and from between the lids shone blue
fire. "You will have the very great
goodness, Monsieur, to remember
these two facts, and hereafter those
to whom I present you, women or
men, trust them whether you trust
them or not."

Late that night in the Baroness's
bedroom, the Baroness's maid, brush-
ing out the shimmering gold and
gray hair, wondered why her mistress
laughed so.

There was a drop of eighty degrees
in Charles Teste's mercury, and in
the change his soul was frozen pure
of assertiveness and rebellion as far as
Talleyrand was concerned. He had
many ways to control men besides

amiability, this wonderful old diplomat, and he knew which to use for whom. Teste, cowed, hurriedly and meekly poured out the most secret workings of his brain; more, of his party. Within a few minutes he had told what regiments were ready to declare for young Napoleon II. — the poor lad now eating his heart out in Vienna, in this spring of 1832; what arsenals would be handed over to the Bonapartists; what civil officials were secretly with them; how the placards would read that were to blossom out on the walls all over Paris; how the very date of the *coup d'état* waited to be fixed only until they were sure of the Duke of Reichstadt's better health. Everything M. Teste knew, and it was much, for he was a great

man in his small way, he told the
little circle, eagerly, anxiously, one
restless eye rolling always toward that
dangerous old face where the smaller
beast of prey recognized his master,
the greater. The recital was finished,
and Teste was silent, shocked and
astonished by his own unreserve. A
clear-headed, tireless organizer, he
was a Bonapartist for two reasons.
His father, a Paris artisan, risen to be
a colonel of a regiment under the
first Napoleon, and with all the son's
intensity, but without his keenness,
had taught him adoration of the
Great Captain from his cradle as his
creed. And the other reason was
that he hated Louis Philippe — Louis
Philippe, who truckled to Russia and
England, who had no sympathy with

the army ; Louis Philippe, who abandoned Belgium and Italy ; who cared
little for the glory of France, if only
the kings called him brother ; who
was yet but a bourgeois King — and
the French love their monarchs to be
royal. In the two years of his reign,
he had managed, this worthy gentleman, to make enemies, sometimes
on very insufficient grounds, of two-
thirds of his subjects. The picturesque figure of the sad young prince
who might have been their young
Emperor, Napoleon II., stood out
from the distant background of his
Austrian prison, and came to many a
Frenchman's mind at that time with
a passionate appeal. From under the
grinding heel of the Bourbons had
come the Revolution, and the people

had summoned their poor, great
strength and torn the fabric of the
monarchy to tatters. It was Napoleon who had gathered up the ragged
threads of those tatters, and woven a
nation, a country again for the French.
And then somehow — how was it?
They hardly knew — his star had
set, he was dead in exile, and here
were the hated Bourbons on the
throne again. And his son, his child,
was prisoner in an Austrian castle.
Should they not bring him back, and
under him drive out the tyrants again?
Yes! Heaven help them, yes! *Vive
l'Empereur!* The child of Napoleon — that thought burned deep into
many a French heart in those days.

The Prince of Benevento leaned
back in Madame's satin chair, his

proudly set old head daintily white against the warm rose color and the gilded wood, and on his lips and through his half-shut eyes gleamed what was called his " perpetual smile." He was thinking, and though they were all bubbling with questions, each one felt that a lion over a bone would be as good to disturb as Talleyrand over a thought. The game was, as always, in his hands, and they waited in deep silence; even the Baroness, who dared much. The Prince's face brightened at last. The clear, light eyes opened wide, and he gazed around him with a smile of child-like affection.

"Ah!" he said, "good, *mon ami — mon cher M. Teste*. I think the machinery will work — when oiled."

And now the keen, smiling face became thoughtful again, and he began
to talk softly as if to himself. " M.
Teste is turning over, in that great
brain of his " — could there be a
mocking tone in that gentle voice?
— " is pondering why I, who plotted
against Napoleon, should be plotting
now to place his heir on France's
throne. ' What is the old rascal
after ? ' they are asking each other.
' What chestnuts are we to pull out
of the fire for that arch-deceiver ? '
Ah, yes ! They question, they puz-
zle, but one thought sends a glow to
their hearts — if Talleyrand is in the
plot the plot is safe. I never con-
spired in my life except when I had
the majority of France as accomplice,
and when " — a look of high dig-

nity replaced the gay mockery on
his face — " when I sought with that
majority the safety of the fatherland.
The King knows," he went on, as if
arguing out the question to himself,
" that I am not dynastic. Since Louis
XVI. I have served all the govern-
ments, out of attachment to my
country. I have abandoned them as
soon as they sacrificed the interests
of France to the interests of individ-
uals. So I abandoned Napoleon. So
will I now abandon Louis Philippe,
whom I serve to-day as Ambassador
to England." A smile like a win-
ning child's suddenly flashed, as if
with irresistible child's mischief, over
the bitter lips. " The pleasant re-
union of this evening is not strictly
in the King's service," he whispered,

confidentially, and everyone laughed with him light-heartedly. Then he changed to a practical tone. " Messieurs, I monopolize the conversation. In my old age I become garrulous. I am seventy-eight years of age, Messieurs, and I have been a little spoiled. Madame, you should not let me become a bore."

The Baroness had long ago come under the spell of that wonderful personality. " Monsieur," she answered, impulsively, " it is the only thing you do not know how to do. I would rather hear you talk than anyone in the world, Monsieur — except myself."

The Baroness could be impertinent and attractive together, and the piquancy of it charmed Talleyrand.

22

"Madame, you are delicious," he said. "How did you learn to be truthful and adorable at once ? Now lend me your clever brain to tell these gentlemen what only you and I fully know as yet. First, we shall tell them — " He turned his enigmatical smile upon her, admiring but cold-blooded, ready to trap her quickly if she failed to read his mind.

But the Baroness's mind was clear and ready, too. " First we shall tell them," she said, "if Monsieur de Talleyrand so pleases, how well all is going ; how the keen eye of M. Teste has overlooked nothing, has grasped the great chances and missed no details ; how the soldierly courage of M. le Général Bertrand has known how to win the army ; how the country has been stirred to memories of Napoleon, to hopes of Napoleon's child; how every combination has been arranged accurately; how, most of all, M. le Prince, who is the other word for Success, is with us heart and soul." She smiled across at Talleyrand. "We will tell them that several times, if you do not mind, Monsieur," and she stopped short.

"Excellently done!" The old minister tapped two fingers lightly on the palm of his other hand. "Messieurs, you have heard our diplomate? I repeat, I indorse it all. The train is laid, the touch of a match and the explosion will put the Duke of Reichstadt — the King of Rome — on his father's throne. And I have certain news this morning," he added, quickly

24

and cheerfully, putting the tips of his hands delicately together, "that the King of Rome cannot live a month."

Sometimes when a bomb falls there is a breathless second of stillness before it bursts and rips the earth and sky. So for a short moment Bertrand and Teste, as motionless as marble, gazed open-mouthed into the smiling, wrinkled face before them. The May breeze through the open windows stirred the curls on the Baroness's forehead, and the sounds of great Paris outside floated in to them across the silence. There was a fountain trickling in the court-yard.

The old General was the first to recover.

"It is impossible!" he gasped. "Impossible! He *must* live! What

25

then can be done? *Mon Dieu! Il faut qu'il*" — and the words tangled themselves ridiculously in their desperate eagerness to be spoken. "It is not his life, it is the life of France — *la patrie!* M. Teste!" He turned with a groan of appeal.

But M. Teste, moistening his lips like a man in anguish, was watching dumbly the inexplicable smile of Talleyrand. He knew well that this man was entirely selfish, calculating, and cold, but would he dare to smile like that if all their hopes, their plans of months, were shipwrecked? He was deeply committed with them. What did this nonchalance mean?

"However," went on the strong, well-bred, even voice, "it is, after all, of little or no importance."

An indignant start shook the General and Teste. The calm voice continued.

"Twenty-one years ago the Emperor provided for such a contingency as has arisen this evening. I have here" — and his hand, moving with the same elegance and daintiness of gesture as if he presented a flower, flung open the velvet of his coat and sought an inner pocket — "I have here certain writings that will serve, I hope, to clear the atmosphere of this meeting, which has been so agreeable to this point, but which I regret to feel has become — thunder-laden, perhaps?" His eyes, quick and masterful, turned to Victor and young Ney. "Messieurs, you have, I believe, copies of these important documents?"

Without a word they laid the yel-
lowed, folded papers, exactly like his
own, in Talleyrand's hand, and without a word he rose, took two halting
steps to a table near Teste and breaking with care the seals, opened the
packets and spread them out. Bertrand and Teste crowded against each
other, bent shoulder to shoulder over
the faded writing. The Baroness
stood, a willowy white figure, poised,
still, but strung to intensity, watching.
Young Ney and Marshal Victor,
knowing the secret, yet breathed fast,
realizing that history was making in
the quiet room. And the club-
footed, lame old man, the master
magician, leaned on his cane, and
smiled again the perpetual smile
through half-closed lids as he looked

with pleased interest at the working of his charms.

The two readers gasped, choked as they read, with trembling fingers laid on the papers, and eyes staring out as if the sight tried to rush forward, to arrive sooner at those undreamed-of words, beneath which ran the straggling signature of the dead Emperor, of Baron Dubois, of Jean Siffrein Maury, Archbishop of Paris. Great as was the magnitude of the fact, it lay in comparatively few words. Soon they had read, they knew; and slowly they raised their eyes, astonished, dazed, to each other's faces. Then the General, shaking all over, turned and stared at Talleyrand like a man in a dream. Twice he tried to speak and failed; suddenly his figure

stiffened to military erectness, his
arm flew above his head as if it waved
a sword, and as if leading a charge, he
shouted :

"*Vive l' Empereur !* " cried the General.

"Vive l'Empereur!" cried the General.

Chapter Two

FAR down the walls of Castle Kilmorra the waves thundered against its rock foundation. In the great hall the master, pulling at his pipe and staring dreamily into the logs that blazed and roared up the chimney, found his memory wandering, guided by the deafening storm, back to the thunder of great battles that long ago, in his youth, had been his best music.

" In his youth ! " He gave a vigorous kick to a rolling log and then settled sinewy elbows on muscular legs and dropped his clean-shaven, fresh face into his strong hands and

stared again at the blaze with eyes as
clear and blue as when the young
Irish officer fought, twenty-five years
before, under the first Napoleon.

Oh, but that was living! People
might call him a tyrant now, and
selfish, and small-souled. It was easy
enough and cheap enough for the
meanest, now that he had died at St.
Helena. But those who served under
him never cared for a reason because
they adored him. There never was
but one Bonaparte, and his memory,
to his followers, was glory and success, and the mad joy of triumphant
battle, a memory that thrilled his
soldiers' pulse to the latest moment
of the longest life. Patrick Fitzgerald had fought in the sunshine of
Austerlitz, had been one of those who

swarmed up the ladder with Marshal
Lannes in the glorious ditch at Ratisbon, and as he sat, twenty-five years
later, a quiet country gentleman, before the great fireplace of his old
home in Ireland, the storm outside
was enough to stir his blood with the
thought of his hero.

Picture after picture flashed, alive
with color and movement and music,
across his brain, always with that
central figure, the Emperor. Then
his heart throbbed suddenly as there
came upon him, from this unaccus-
tomed avenue of thought, a memory
that had been his familiar, every-
day companion for over twenty years.
How could it be true? How could
it be that the greatest soldier of the
world, the leader of mighty armies,

the robed and ermined figure whom
he had seen place the crown on his
own head that day in Notre Dame
— that Napoleon should have put
such a trust in the hands of simple
Captain Fitzgerald, who had little
but his old Irish name and his gay
Irish courage.

Yet he could not very well have
dreamed it. He went over it all
again, the events of that strange
night in late March of the year
1811. He saw the heavy, pale-blue
satin hangings in the Palace of the
Tuileries, and heard the deep voices
of his fellow-officers as they sat at
cards around a table till the early
morning light came creeping in.
Again and again and again he had
gone over the least details, so that

when his recollection reached Beauregard's face as he threw double aces,
and the tones of his gay voice, saying,
" *Dites donc*, Fitzgerald, *mon brave* ;
they say you have a fourth son to-
day " — instantly he heard also the
heavy boom of a cannon.

How they had started, the Frenchmen ! And then sat frozen in their
chairs, each man holding his hand
lifted or lowered, as if the stir of
a finger could drown the gun that
was telling Paris of the birth of
the Emperor's child. One man
spoke quickly — " Twenty-one for a
daughter, one hundred for a son " —
and they frowned at him ; they all
knew it.

" Nineteen " — it was Beauregard
who began to count aloud — " twenty,

twenty-one." The reverberations died slowly, and the officers listened intently for the next heavy boom, and then, as it did not come, drew long breaths and looked at each other, and Beauregard again, always the first to speak, threw up his hands.

"A girl, then! Ah, kind Fate, for the Emperor's sake, another gun! If the twenty-second might but sound!" And, as he spoke, it sounded.

The guns went on merrily then, and nobody counted, but they all drank, and drank again, to the young King of Rome, to the Empress, to the great Emperor. Fitzgerald was standing on the table, expounding a flowery toast in fine Irish-flavored

English, which nobody understood but all cheered madly, when the door opened, and Constant, the Emperor's valet, came in. They all knew him, and there was silence instantly, for his coming must mean a message from Napoleon.

" M. le Capitaine Fitzgerald ? " suggested Constant, inquiringly, his fox-face looking about as if he did not know his man ; and Fitzgerald, standing, with his feet in their great cuirassier boots, among the cards on the polished table, his glass still in his hand, owned to his name.

" His Majesty the Emperor desires the presence of M. le Capitaine in his cabinet."

And Fitzgerald, rather dazed, climbed down from the table and

followed Constant to the interview
that had been the astonishment and
the glory, shared by no other soul,
of his life. There were others who
knew, three of them — Napoleon
had told him that — but he did not
know their names, and they had given
no sign. He should never know,
unless — he looked down at his hand
where the firelight sparkled on a ring
— "unless France should need her."
He repeated the words to himself.

A door opened at the farther end
of the hall, and three strapping young
men came in, blue-eyed and fresh-
colored, lean and big-boned, like the
lord of the castle, evidently his sons.
They came to the fire and sat down
around him like three young brothers,
a hand on his shoulder in passing, a

mischievous tip of his chair, showing
the affectionate and familiar terms
they were all on together. Colonel
Fitzgerald, shaking off his revery,
glanced at them with satisfied pride.
They were the sort he liked, handsome and strong and plucky — fine
Irish gentlemen, with good-nature
and a twinkle of humor besides
showing plain in the eye of each.

" How goes the new pipe, Colonel? " asked Alex, the oldest. " It
ought to be something wonderful
after coming all the way from London, or never hold up its head again."

" By post, too, lad," added Dennis.
" Remember it posted to Dublin —
no mere travelling by mail. At
Sackville Street it alighted, they say,
and led Lord Kilkenny, strongly

against his will, to the bar of —
what's the name of the place? —
where it treated him right nobly to
various strong drinks, to the health
of the land of punch, priests, and
potatoes, for which he paid the
charge."

"It's a way it has," said Patrick,
Jr. "Once see that pipe, and you
may look with faith around the cor-
ner for the punch — ah! it's got
here, I notice," and he rolled an eye
toward a side-table where stood a
bowl and glasses.

"Peg away, lads," said the Colonel,
placidly, looking at the pipe which
he held in the palm of his hand.
"You're all jealous. It's a good
pipe, and it's a fine trick Lord Kilkenny has of bringing one every

year from London. Faith, I would n't
have him disturbed in the habit for
worlds. Where's Norah?" he asked.

"With Whirlwind, of course."

"Nothing wrong with Whirlwind,
is there?"

"No, I think not. But the saddle slipped a bit to-day and rubbed
half of a hair off his withers, and
Miss Norah must see to it herself.
Shamus was n't to be trusted, and by
the same token, no more was I,"
said Alex. "So off she went to the
stables. I would n't grieve my heart
out if Whirlwind should set up a
small uninjurious malady for a few
days. The girl's going to hurt herself with her mad riding."

The Colonel laughed. "Not
Norah. She knows horses as you

boys will never know them," he said, proudly, and the lads looked pleased too. " Not but what you 're good horsemen, but Norah has a knack that 's a miracle. It 's the same with men," he added, musingly. " She holds up the tip of her finger and she smiles at them, and it 's a pleasure to upset all plans for her. It was the same — " He stopped, staring at the fire. Dennis finished the sentence for him : " With her father, you were thinking, I 'll wager a hat, Colonel."

The young men laughed. But Colonel Fitzgerald turned and looked at them queerly.

" It was my thought," he said, without a smile.

The merry youngsters stopped, a

bit puzzled. Alex, harking back, said, seriously: "Well, then, Norah may be all that's wonderful, and I'm proud to think she is, but upon my soul she takes risks. You ought to caution her, father. Devil a bit of attention she'll pay to anyone else, and she does n't know what fear means."

Dennis joined in. "Yesterday, when Lord Kilkenny brought over the pipe —" "Rest its sowl," interjected Patrick in broad Irish, but Dennis went on gravely — "he told me that he saw her take the sunk fence on the Gurt na brocha, and you know it's safe for no horse in this soft weather. Whirlwind's back feet had n't an inch to spare, he said. And she caught a cropper a week ago

43

— you never knew it. Whirlwind refused the wall by the Curryglass farm, and she put him at it again and he took it low, and they spilled. Norah was up and pulling at his bridle before Shamus could get to her, and she ordered Shamus not to tell, but I came on him doctoring the horse where he cut his side, and I got it from him."

Colonel Fitzgerald pulled at his pipe. "The horse wasn't hurt?" he asked.

"Only a scratch. It's the girl I'm afraid for," said Alex.

"I'm not afraid for her," said the Colonel. "But I'll speak to her. Yet I doubt if — it's the blood that's in her," he said in a low voice, shaking his head.

44

"It 's your blood, Colonel, and ours," said Dennis. " And I 'll wager I could order a girl to do my bidding, and make her do it, too, if I were her father," he went on, tossing his tow-head. And just then, " Toot-toot-a-too-too," from the very threshold of the room a bugle blew — loud and strong on the first notes, a pitiful bleat at the end — and the proud Dennis and all the others started violently and turned to stare at the door.

There a red- and shame-faced groom stood, much alarmed, holding the instrument which had just dropped from his still open mouth, and just behind him, half in the shadow, a military figure — that is, until you noticed that the cocked

45

hat and officer's coat were finished illogically by a tweed skirt that marred the war-like effect. But a gallant-looking young soldier it was, all the same, that strode toward the group.

"Right-about — forward — left flank — march — company — sit down," and down she sat on the knee of Colonel Fitzgerald and gave him a mad hug and a kiss on his head and a tug at his left ear. From this strategic position she then issued orders to her trembling army in the rear.

"You may go back to your horses now, Shamus O'Shaughnessy. You're a good, obedient boy, and though you've the courage of a small cat I'm pleased with you.

46

Fly!" And Shamus, as well as he could, for shivering and shaking, flew.

"Daddy, look at me," and she hugged him again, making it quite impossible to look at anything. Then she sprang to her feet. "Attention, men! Daddy, it's the living image of yourself I am, as you fought under the Great Captain. Boys dear, you hulking Irishmen, tell me I'm not like my father now, if you can — you who are always jeering me for a dark foreigner."

"Faith," said Dennis, "you're the living image of someone, but I can't place my hand on his name."

"It's a big name you're looking for," said Alex, quietly, "for it's Napoleon."

Colonel Fitzgerald started and turned a keener glance on the girl, and the blood rushed over his face and up into his eyes.

" The lad is right. It 's himself," he said, through his teeth.

" Me ? " said Norah, glancing brightly from one to another. " I am like the Great Captain ? Look, then, daddy — did n't he stand like this at Ratisbon ? " She threw her head forward, hands clasped behind, and out of her gray eyes shot the very look of the Conqueror, mixed with youthful mischief. A short curl had blown loose in front and fell on her broad forehead, beneath the three-cornered hat. The likeness was unmistakable.

The young Fitzgeralds laughed

" Look, then, daddy—didn't he stand like this at Ratisbon? "

and exclaimed, but their father, springing to his feet, gazed at the girl and shook with emotion.

"Norah — my little Norah," he gasped. And in a second one of the soldierly arms was around his neck, and the cocked hat lay on his breast.

"Why, daddy, I did n't know it would bother you. I won't do it again. No, never! Wait, then." She drew away from his arms, and in a second the cocked hat and the coat with its gorgeous facings lay in a disrespectful heap on the floor.

"Now I'm your Irish Norah again, and it's all I wish to be. It was you I wanted to look like, daddy, not the Emperor. The Emperor's nothing to me, but it

4   49

worries me to have the boys say I'm
the only one who's not a red Fitzgerald. I'm as good a Fitzgerald
as any man of them all. Tell them
I am, daddy."

"Boys, you're not to be hinting
but she's as good a Fitzgerald as
the lot of you together," said the
Colonel, smiling again.

"Better — tell them I'm better,
father," coaxed Norah. "Insult them
for me, father; it's pleasant to see
them insulted, the great, blundering
— darling boys," and she flew at
Patrick and Dennis, as they stood
side by side, and cracked their big
heads together before they had time
to resist.

"Now, you little lambs, don't you
bother this great black wolf again,"

she said, and cocked her head at the three tall fellows.

The distant door of the room opened cautiously, and Tim, the butler, put in his dignified gray head with the look of an arch conspirator.

" Colonel, darlin'."

" Go away, Tim. Leave the room ; leave the country. Go to heaven," said Norah, facing about toward him.

" Sure, then, Miss Norah," pleaded Tim.

" The Colonel *won't* see you. Is n't it plain to be seen we 're having a family quarrel and we want to enjoy it in peace ? Have you no delicacy, Tim — you, with your big eyes, as if you had kings and princes waiting behind you, and all you want is to ask whether we'll have carrots or turnips to-morrow for dinner?"

"Sure, Miss Norah," said Tim, helplessly, and rolled an entreating eye toward Colonel Fitzgerald — "sure if you'll lave me shpake, Colonel, before I starts for heaven afther Miss Norah's marchin' orders — an' it's good luck she's not ordered me to the other place, for I'd have to go," with a grin — "sure there's three sthrange gintle-min waitin' to shpake wid yez."

"What is it you're saying, Tim?" said Colonel Fitzgerald, lazily. "There can't be strangers come to Kilmorra a night like this? You're always a play-actor. You'll be

52

telling me next it's fairy princes, blown in by the thunder, you have down there."

"Sure an' they're that sort," said Tim, in a stage whisper, leaning forward with bright, scared eyes. "'Tis the great lords from foreign parts, they'll be, sure, Colonel dear, and they're all rich wid furs an' jools, an' they shpake the lingo."

"French?" asked Fitzgerald, tersely. Tim had been with him through the wars.

Tim nodded. "'Tis that, sor. I should know it like the swish of the swords."

The Colonel stood up, holding the arms of his chair, and looked around at his children. The color and glow went slowly out of his face, and left the skin hanging yellow on his large bony features.

"It's come," he said, "France needs her."

There was a silence while the young people stared at him astonished, and then the blood and the courage found Colonel Fitzgerald's heart again.

"Children, dear, you'd better leave me," he said. "Tim, bring the gentlemen to me here."

Chapter Three

A CLEAN rush of light hoofs on the turf behind the wall, and over they came, horse and girl, a vision of life and color, of powerful and graceful strength. To Michael Ney, in his saddle at the side of the road, it seemed as if they rose twenty feet in the air, and soared as birds soar, without effort, before the water-jump was cleared, and Whirlwind came down, crazy with glee and excitement, and was a hundred yards off across the field by the time the laughing girl who sat him could pull him in.

55

" Is n't he the pretty jumper ? " she called, as they turned, horse and rider together, and cantered lightly back.

But Michael was so absorbed in looking at the picture coming to him across the wide, sky-topped greenness that he forgot to answer — hardly heard the question. The finest sight on earth is a good horse with a good rider ; and young Ney, looking at these two with a trained eye, knew that each was of the best. The horse was a light-built black, quick as a kitten, full of fire and full of nerve, with a dancing step that seemed just to touch ; slim legs, a small, proud head, and a pair of eyes that told much — wild, restless, and flashing they were ; and when the

little ears went back close, and those
dark, blood-shot eyes gleamed at you,
you felt why the grooms and even the
young Fitzgeralds called Whirlwind
dangerous. You realized that he
would carry his master till his heart
broke, if need be, and might well kill
a rider, too, who was not his master.
But as he came up now across the
field, though exhilarated from the
leap and eager for more excitement,
and though the girl on his back sat
loose and held the reins lightly in
one hand as she bent to pat his neck,
Whirlwind was quite under control.

"How lovely she is!" Michael
thought. He had seen prettier girls,
without doubt, for she was no regu-
lation beauty, but none in his life
with this girl's fascination — full of

mischief and gayety, unexpected at
every turn, yet with a dignity that
encased her as the air encases the
earth ; with a will and a courage to
sway an army, and yet innocent and
good and gentle, loving enthusiasti-
cally her simple life with the brothers
and the father who were her humble
servants and whom she adored ; a life
like a mountain-stream rushing impetuously, musically down between
hills, bright with sunlight, and sweet
with quiet shadows; breaking bravely,
and with foamy laughter, over the
rocks in its path, and sparkling
through the monotony of the shal-
lows ; each drop fresh and alive
under every sort of sky — a life that
might well, some day, thought the
young man, widen into a strong and

stately river, the artery of a nation. He had been left at Castle Kilmorra partly to study her character, and this was what he was making of it.

"Whirlwind mavourneen, poor beast, faith, we must do it — there's nothing else left," and she bent toward the horse's flicking ears. "It's hard to die so young and so suddenly and in such good hunting country, too, but we must do it, I fear."

"What sad secret are you telling Whirlwind, Miss Norah?" asked Michael, wheeling his horse beside hers as she came up.

"It's the custom of the family, that's all. When a Fitzgerald's heart is broken, it's the custom to ride off Castle Rock, to save bother."

"Is your heart broken, then? What villain has done it?"

"Just you," said Norah, looking at him mournfully from her deep eyes. "Whirlwind's heart, too. Speak up, Whirlwind dear, and tell him you're suffering," and she gave the horse a sudden thump with the butt end of her whip that made him leap six feet and snort angrily. Norah laughed and tossed her head.

"It's the spirit that's in you that I love you for, Whirlwind," she said; "for all you're broken-hearted." Then she gathered herself and her horse and faced Michael like a general reviewing his troops.

"What sort of a Frenchman do you call yourself, to let Whirlwind and me be leaping sunk fences and

VIVE L'EMPEREUR

things for you, and never give us the
smallest word of a compliment that
ever was — and us perishing for a bit
of blarney. That's why my heart is
broken." She frowned darkly at him.

" You and Whirlwind stole my
heart from me a week ago, Miss
Norah," said the young man, a touch
too seriously. " I think the pieces
of that, if there are any left, might
serve to patch yours — I doubt if
it's badly injured. As for Whirlwind, I'll patch his with a lump of
sugar when we get home. And as
for the compliment, if you knew the
words I was busy keeping my tongue
from saying, you would not dare ask
me to let it loose."

Norah looked up at him with
pleased eyes.

"R-r-really ? " she asked, the Irish
r rolling sweetly. "Now that's very
pretty. You're forgiven, sir. Faith,
you're a real Irishman, for all your
French name."

"I wonder if you suspect that
you're a real Frenchwoman, for all
your Irish name ? " retorted Michael,
looking down at her, as they trotted
side by side.

"Not that," said Norah, quickly.
"I'm not that. I don't mean to be
rude," with a friendly glance over at
him, "but the boys bother me that
way — telling me I'm foreign and
dark and not like the fair Fitzgeralds,
when I'm proud of being a good
Irishwoman above everything else."

"I have Irish blood, too, Miss
Norah, and not so far back," said

Michael, gently. "And I love old Ireland, too. Heavens! I love it!" He took off his hat and shook his light hair loose and drew a long breath as he gazed at the beautiful landscape, as if to drink in the green- ness and the fresh beauty of it. "Yet it is my pride to be a Frenchman," he added, slowly. "And it is my hope in life to strike a blow for France some day — God helping me!" The fresh, strong young face stared off at the horizon, full of fire and solemnity.

"But I need n't bother you with heroics — yet," he said, and smiled down at her.

"It 's a *drôle* of a Frenchman you are, as father would say," said Norah. "A patriot to your finger-tips, and

yet you are big and blond like an
Irishman or a Scotchman, and you
speak English like — well, there,
now — it is n't quite like an Englishman, either, but surely not like a
Frenchman. How do you come to
be so queer, then?"

Michael laughed, but as if his own
peculiarities interested him less than
the girl's evident interest in them.
" I 'll explain myself if you wish it,
Miss Norah. My father, who had
both Scotch and Irish blood, was
always taken for a Scotchman in his
young days," he said. " My color
and height come from him. And
as for my English — I don't speak
like an Englishman, then?" he asked,
curiously.

" It 's this way," said Norah.

"Did you ever hear of my father's friend Captain O'Flaherty, of Dublin? It was he complained that his French always showed him to be English, and his English proved him to be Irish. But I don't know what your English proves you to be," and she scrutinized him thoughtfully. "For it's not Irish and it's not quite English. There's a manner of softness about it, and you slip over the *r*'s as if they were n't there. And some syllables you'll make a yard long, while the others you'll take half a dozen to the jump. I don't know what it is at all — tell me, then." She looked at him, and instead of the amused, laughing look she expected, his face wore a grave expression, his eyes gazed down

5   65

thoughtfully at the pommel of the saddle.

"Miss Norah, if you care really to hear about it, I 'll tell you more gladly than anyone in the world. It is a secret of history — and even history may never know it — that lies at the bottom of so small a thing as my accent. You know who I am ? Or, rather, for that 's nothing, whose son I am ? "

"The son of the great Marshal Ney — of him the Emperor called ' the bravest of the brave,' " said Norah, reverently and softly, looking at him with eyes that made his heart go fast.

Michael shifted his bridle, put his left hand on Whirlwind's mane and fixed his gaze on the girl's face. "You know he was supposed to be shot after Waterloo? Louis XVIII. ordered it, and the execution, or the form of it, was carried out in the early morning of December 7, 1815, in an alley behind the Luxembourg. But there was a plot — I might give you all the details and the names, for they are burned into my brain, but I will not now. It is enough to tell you that the plot had aid from very high quarters — the Duke of Wellington himself, who was in Paris with the allied armies, knew of it. The file of soldiers who were detailed to shoot him were of my father's old command — that was arranged. As he passed them, his own old veterans, he whispered, ' Fire high ' — his last order before a battle had always been, ' Fire low.' "

Suddenly Michael stopped and stared at Norah as if appalled. She sat her horse like a statue, her lips were closed tight, and her eyes flashed gray fire. " My God," whispered Michael, awed, " the likeness! "

She turned her eyes to his quickly. " Go on," she ordered, and her breath came fast.

He went on. " My father gave the word ' Fire,' and fell. Then they fired — over him. The rest was easy. He was taken to a hospital and from there to Bordeaux and from there he sailed to America. I think it is the most wonderful secret in all history," said the young fellow, his face flushed with deep feeling, his shining eyes still on Norah's excited face. " A hundred people

" My God," whispered Michael, awed, "the likeness!"

must have known it, in a vague way
all France knew it, for the people
have never believed him dead, and
yet the Government never found out
— no one was ever punished for helping him escape." Then in a quiet
voice he went on: "I have lived
many years, though not all of my
life, with my father in America, in
the South, in a State called Virginia,
where he has bought a large place —
thousands of acres. He is what they
call a planter. That is all. Now
you see why I speak English differ-
ently from Irishmen and English-
men. It is the accent of America,
of the South."

Norah drew a long, trembling
breath. "I don't care about that.
Don't bother me about your accent

now. I am thinking of that dark winter morning in Paris, and those good old soldiers, drawn up to shoot at their own great general who had led them into battle. Great heavens! You must think of it always! You must live in that memory! No wonder you are different from other people!" And she turned to him with a sudden movement that made him thrill — with that and the fire of her look, impersonal though it was.

"Am I different?" asked Michael. It was hard to speak at all when she looked at him like that.

Norah turned her head away rather hurriedly. "Oh, yes, quite," she said in a business-like tone that was ice-water on fire. Then she went on,

"1815 — were you old enough to realize?"

"I was seven," said Michael. "I don't think I realized very much, but I missed my father greatly. It was for that reason they sent me to him — I grieved for him so that it made me ill. I had two older brothers who were more important — they have the titles — so my mother could spare me. And he needed me in his exile — it is an exile still, for he longs for France always."

"Can he never come back?" asked Norah. Michael turned a look full of meaning upon her. "When there is again a Bonaparte on the throne — yes," he said.

"And is that to be?" asked Norah eagerly. "Is something going to

happen, then? Is that why you and
the Prince and the Marshal came to
Kilmorra? But why should you
come to Kilmorra? Is it because
my father is a great soldier and you
want him and the boys for leaders?
Is there to be a *coup d'état*, as father
has said was sure to be some day?
Are they going to make the King of
Rome Emperor?"

Michael smiled and looked at her
a moment, then turned away his eyes,
as if afraid to trust them.

"A fine lot of state questions
you've piled into a sentence or two,
Miss Norah." Then his face grew
serious again. "Your right to know
all about it is far greater than mine,"
he said, "and soon you will know.
Yet at present I'm not allowed to

talk freely to you, and you're coming close to the heart of things." He turned a look of longing on her puzzled face that she could not understand.

"Come, now, there's a fine soft road for a run. I'll wager the Saint will beat Whirlwind to the cabins up yonder, and all by clever jockeying." And off they went, pell-mell, the white and the black spinning up the road in a staccato chorus of sparkling hoofs.

Chapter Four

SO for three weeks Norah Fitzgerald and Michael rode in the
June weather about the lanes
of County Clare, and meanwhile the
history of a nation, the fate of a
coup d'état, hung on their riding.
Many a career was marred, many another had its chance of being, only
because of the light in Norah's eyes
and the answering light in Michael's
before the word that matched it came.
The keenest joy of companionship is
to feel another mind catch the flame
of your own across the space of silence. Day by day he could see her

count more surely on his understand-
ing her thoughts, and turn to him
with a shade of laughter that even
father and brothers missed. His
mind, travelling swiftly to meet hers,
often brought up with an electric
shock to find her there, just outside
the very doorway of his thought.
Every day to the impetuous, strong-
willed, warm-hearted Michael Ney
it grew a dearer luxury, a nearer ne-
cessity, this quick, sweet touch of
souls — almost more than the touch
of her hand it thrilled him. Every
night when he went to his room,
after a day spent assiduously in wrong-
doing, he lectured himself with
shame and pain.

"To-morrow shall be different,"
he vowed. " I have no right — no

right " — and sometimes he finished
the sentence and whispered aloud —
" no right to love her." Often he
tossed the question impatiently aside
with the thought, " After all, I am
the only one to suffer. She is light-
hearted and free-hearted. She shall
never know this." And all the time
every look was telling her.

Ah, why had they chosen him to
stay there, of the three ? He knew
well enough the reason — that someone should be at hand when the
great event came ; that Talleyrand,
Ambassador to England, must be at
his post in London ; that the old
Marshal's English was impossible ;
that he, to all appearances simply a
young American gentleman, could
rouse no suspicions. But could n't

they have seen — could n't a blind
man have seen—the danger? Wasn't
he made to love her? And now he
must hold his peace and go through
with this horrible, picturesque, melo-
dramatic business, and with his own
hands help to put her forever beyond
his reach. Michael's eager soul
longed to throw off the artificial
right and wrong of it, and sweep her
up fiercely—a laughing, high-spirited,
willing Norah — and carry her off
to the ends of the world.

Ride after ride; on shadowy, wet
mornings, when the pale greenness
was a mist, with no outlines, only a
gracious, dewy melting of hedges and
walls and trees into one soft landscape;
on glorious afternoons, when the
land was emerald — a gold and green

world, with bouquets of pink and white thorn set here and there — and they rode with their heads close to the fairy freshness of the boughs; once or twice coming home in the early moonlight, when it seemed as if they were a knight and a lady of long ago, riding through a dim old story of King Arthur.

From the saddle the picture of the world about is seen at another angle, and the difference, the surprise, never fails. Each time you mount you go up into a new, fresh country; each day's weather has a new master-word, a delicious secret that is whispered in your ear only, and that you can never tell, for there are no words that will say it.

The two, as they rode out daily

into the beautiful unexpectedness, felt each a restful certainty that the other understood; which, considering the position they were scheduled to occupy towards each other, was a dangerous state of things. One night they halted their horses on the crest of a high hill. There were miles of country spread out below, around them. Leagues of sky seemed to bend over and touch them. The stars and the lights of the village of Scattery, far below, began to gleam together out of the misty twilight. Beyond rolled the ocean.

"Is there anybody in the world but us two?" asked Michael, looking back from the wide, still landscape toward Norah—and Whirlwind took a restless step that jostled her

shoulder against his. Quick as
thought — quicker than his thought
— he bent down and kissed the sleeve
that touched him, and then, pale
with feeling, frightened at himself,
he stared at her. Norah's eyes were
fixed on her hands, and the hands
trembled. As if under a spell, the
two sat so for a moment, still as
death.

Then it was Michael who said,
speaking with difficulty: "I think
we had better go home," and all the
three miles of the road back Whirlwind led a mad race, and Norah
waved her whip and urged him on
across shadowy ditches and over dim
hedges, recklessly. At the table she
kept father and brothers in a peal of
laughter from beginning to end of

the meal. And Michael, watching miserably to catch her glance, could never once do it, for it danced cheerfully over and past and around him without giving him one straight, friendly look. In look and in speech she treated him to a sparkling feast of diamonds, which, as diamonds can, cut.

His one thought was to see her alone, for five minutes even, to beg her pardon, to straighten out somehow, anyhow, this wretched coil between them. He ached feverishly till that could be done; he must make her understand how sorry, how unhappy, how reverent — he planned the explanation a thousand ways.

But when he tried to draw her outside, into the moonlight, she

6

threw her arm around Colonel Fitzgerald's big shoulder and vowed he
should go and look at the moon on
the sea, too — it was good for him
— he had no sense of beauty — it
was training for his finer qualities he
needed. And the three great boys
stalked after them, while Michael
boiled and fumed to get into the
house again.

The next day went in much the
same way. When Michael suggested
a ride, Patrick and Dennis must ride
with them, the blessed boys; she had
not seen them, to speak of, for weeks.
But that night Michael grew cun-
ning, and started the Colonel and his
sons, Alex being of an argumentative
turn, on a fiery discussion of Euro-
pean politics. And Miss Norah, who

cared little for such things and was no patient listener, slipped out shortly by the side door that led to the old garden. And when she was gone no more than three minutes Michael stood up, and said, smilingly:

"Miss Norah and I have had a quarrel, Colonel Fitzgerald. She misunderstood me a little, and by your leave I'm going out to find her and make friends." The Colonel looked at him absentmindedly, his soul on his politics, and said, "Quite right; quite right, my lad," and hammered back at Alex's last argument with no further notice.

So Michael stole out into the moon-lighted, sweet-scented, large, old garden, walking quietly on the turf that bordered the beds of flowers.

He saw her far down by an old sundial, and her arms were on it, and her head on them. His heart beat hard.

"She is n't crying," he said; "she's sleepy. I'm sure she's only sleepy." And then, "I'm going to beg her pardon for touching her. I'm going to tell her I had no right, and I'll never do it again."

He kept saying that to himself, to remember it, as he drew near her.

He stood by her at last, close, in the silvery, quiet night, and as she lifted up her startled face, there were tears on it, and — he forgot.

Chapter Five

IT might have been minutes, or
weeks, after — they neither of
them knew for a certainty —
when suddenly the forgotten world
reappeared in the person of Dennis,
fortunately blind and stupid and much
irritated by not finding them at once,
who bawled out, some six feet away:
"Norah! Mr. Ney! Where the
devil have you got to?" It appeared
that the Prince and the Marshal had
come, unexpectedly as before; that
something had happened, Dennis was
not clear what, but he thought the
Pope was dead; that he did n't care
what it was at all, anyway, only that

he had been sent for Norah and Mr.
Ney, and had been much bothered
to find them, and they were wanted
immediately.

So back they went reluctantly,
guiltily — though only Michael knew
cause for guiltiness — with flushed
cheeks and shining eyes, into the
broad light of the great hall.   There
was a dramatic hush over the five
men who rose as Dennis and his con-
voy entered, and Norah's greeting,
gayer and more voluble because of
embarrassment, was received with a
reverent solemnity that astonished
her.

"My little Norah," said Colonel
Fitzgerald, "dear child of my heart,
if not of my blood, I have very great
news to tell you to-night."

Norah's glance swept the visitors,
paused for a second at her sweetheart's
eyes, and then back to the Colonel.

"Yes, father," was all she said.

Colonel Fitzgerald's big hands
were trembling as he placed one on
Norah's slender shoulder. "You
know well that I've loved you all
your life, darling — better even, I
think, than I love — your brothers?"

"Yes, father." Norah's eyes were
fixed on his face now as if she would
never take them away.

"Then, Norah, my own little
daughter, remember that I love you
more than all your life before, when
I tell you that — " his voice trembled
— "that you are not my child at
all."

Norah's eyes looked into his, wide-open, questioning, but she said not a word.

"These gentlemen are come, my darling, to bring you a great fortune, a great responsibility, and you must meet it and take it up like a brave lady, as you are. A nation needs my little girl, they tell me. France wants you, mavourneen, and France has the right, for you are the only child of Napoleon."

No gleam, no faintest suspicion, had ever come to Norah of the truth. All her world seemed reeling about her. But she stood steady and self-reliant while the circle of men watched. The Prince smiled with satisfaction as he saw her face the shock. The old Marshal said aloud :

"Behold the race! The world is not too large for that lion-bred to hold easily in the hand."

In a moment her clear mind sought to brush away the mist that was nearest. "The King of Rome — the Duke of Reichstadt? You said 'only child.'"

"The King of Rome, poor boy, was — is — my son," said the Colonel, slowly. "He was born a day earlier than you, Norah; and when the Emperor found you were a girl, while his whole heart was set on a boy heir to his throne, he sent for me, darling, and — and you and the boy changed places. My wife, as you know, died when the baby was two days old. The deception was easy. And I did n't know which was the greater

honor, Norah, to have my son brought
up to fill the throne of France, or to
be given the great Captain's child —
to be trusted with the daughter of
Napoleon. I'd have given my life
for the Emperor, gladly, and the lad
was but a day old. And I got you —
Norah."

The Colonel stopped short, his
voice gone, shaken with feeling, far
more sad than joyful over this glorious
transformation of his changeling, and
drew the girl close, while his lips
quivered vainly for more speech.

Marshal Victor, warm-hearted and
emotional, glorying like a Frenchman in the dramatic effect of the
scene, touched with old memories,
with sympathy for the Colonel, sobbed
aloud. Talleyrand looked at him,

considered a second, then shook out
the fine folds of a cambric handker-
chief, and touched his eyes gently
with it. It was the correct effect.
But the old statesman's heart was joyful within him. This last plot of his
long career bid fair to crown that
career with the most successful, the
most picturesque of all *coups d'état*
that he had known. The business
end in France was going well, in
hands that he controlled; the boy at
Vienna was dying at just the right
moment; as for the girl — the Empress — that secret smile of his broad-
ened into real pleasure as he looked
at her, standing among the tall men
grouped about her. The Prince of
Benevento was a connoisseur. Many
women had loved him, and he, affec-

tionate, sweet-tempered, magnetic,
heartless, and self-centred, admired
them all, believed in none of them.

"A woman once loved me truly,"
he said one day to the Baroness.

"Which one, M. le Prince?"
laughed the Baroness.

Talleyrand turned eyes on her at
once keen, mischievous, pathetic. "It
was my great-grandmother," he said.

At all events, he had the readiest
appreciation for a woman's qualities,
and here — it seemed too good to be
true, even for Talleyrand's almost un-
varying good-fortune. The girl was
everything that could be desired —
she bore a likeness to the Emperor
that would convince the nation at
once, and she herself was perfect.
She had spirit, charm, intelligence,

beauty — she would carry the impressionable Frenchmen — all France — by storm ! And then — a glow of satisfaction warmed his soul — then ! A picturesque, charming, pliable young sovereign on the throne, who should lead her and guide her young footsteps in the right way ? Who but he who had placed her so high, Charles Maurice de Talleyrand-Périgord ? What a pleasant, a glorious work to occupy the last days of an eventful life — and not an impoverishing labor, he meditated with a cheerful thought of a golden flood that might be added to a fortune already immense. The tall old man stood half in the shadow of the heavy oak carvings of the fireplace, and watched and thought and smiled.

But at the right second he took up the reins again. He limped forward toward the others. "My Colonel," he said, "but it is a great error to be sad on so joyful an occasion! No one feels more than I for the heart of a father — " his voice trembled just enough — " but while you do not lose your child, we — all France — we gain an Empress." He turned his quick, fascinating eyes on Norah. "Permit an old man, your Highness, an old servant of your illustrious father, the honor to be the first, on this great day of your young life, to offer my felicitations, my allegiance, my life, if need be, to your father's daughter," and taking the girl's hand he bowed low over it and kissed it.

Then, to the surprise of everyone, who but Alex — sober, well-balanced, responsible Alex— should spring forward and, falling on his knee by the Prince, should kiss the small hand passionately.

"Sister darling, many will have more to give, but I will give life and dare death for you, and guard you through danger as best I can."

Norah bent over quickly and her hands swept the thick blond hair and lifted the scarlet face.

"Alex," she said, and kissed him hard on his yellow head. Then as he rose she turned to the strangers and her eyes were full of tears. "There's much to hear," she said; "I must understand much more."

"Her Highness has reason," exclaimed the Marshal, nodding his head wisely. The Prince was silent, puzzled a little by her manner. There was an air of weighing them in the balance about this young Princess that disturbed him slightly. What if — but no, at twenty-one no woman has a will of her own.

"M. Ney," said the Marshal, "I speak not well the English, and we are old, I and M. le Prince — we have not known so much the Princess. You, who speak, you who have the advantage to be young, to be her Highness's friend, there are three week — you will make part of this so great affair to her Highness. You will about to explain to her, how she, she — be Empress." Dignified and earnest, but exhausted with conversational effort, the General sank into a high-colored silence.

M. de Talleyrand turned to the young man. " Go on, *mon ami.* You will know how, as M. le Maréchal says. You have earned well your right to the pleasure. "

Michael, the color rushing to his face, looked about like a hunted beast of the forest. He to explain to her, before this audience! Come, that was too much! He to point out carefully and with congratulations how she was as much out of his reach as the stars; the tragedy of his life — to turn the lights on it with his own hand here before them all! He had braced himself to endure this scene, and that he could just see his way to doing. But to lead the

7   97

attack on his own happiness — how
could he?

Suddenly Norah, who had en-
throned herself — taken refuge — it
was hard to say which, on the arm
of Colonel Fitzgerald's chair, broke
into laughter so infectious that all the
men laughed with her, not knowing
at all what it was about. Even the
Prince of Benevento, watching her
with pleased eyes, was laughing softly,
too.

"It is you, Mr. Ney," she said,
and nodded at Michael's despairing
face.

"It is that it is the thought of the
English, so impayable, him gives a
crise de nerfs," said the General smiling, pleased to think how well he
was doing the language himself.

The laughter cleared the air. Michael all at once found himself unreasonably happy again. She loved him, they understood each other — what was everything else? How could he help being happy? He looked straight into her eyes, which answered his honestly, sweetly, and began:

"Miss Norah — Mademoiselle — your Highness — " Norah almost laughed again — "what no one seems to have told you is that the death of the King of Rome, or the Duke of Reichstadt, as he is now called, is expected at any moment. That death will make you the undisputed, as you have always been the rightful, heir to the French throne. M. le Prince will explain to you far better than

I, when the time comes for fuller explanation, why it is that France wishes once more to throw off the Bourbon yoke, to dethrone the present King, Louis Philippe. It is a fact, however, that the present government is causing deep and widespread discontent. Those with their hands on the nation's pulse say that the time is ripe for a change. The friends of your great father have been secretly organizing for a year with a view to being ready, when the right moment came, to place his child on the throne. The truth of that child's identity has been known, until within a few weeks, to only three persons besides your — Colonel Fitzgerald. To M. de Talleyrand, M. le Maréchal Victor — " Michael bowed with reverence as he spoke each of the great names — "and to my father, the Emperor intrusted, providing for such a crisis as this, duplicate proofs of your identity, signed by himself, by Baron Dubois, the court physician who was present at your birth, by the Archbishop of Paris, who baptized you at the Tuileries when you were twelve hours old. There can be no question of your parentage, my Princess. The proofs are complete."

"I should like to see them," Norah interrupted. Even Talleyrand stared. A young lady who needed to be convinced of her right to be an Empress — *sacre bleu!*

"Yes, your Highness," said Michael, a bit sadly. "But to-morrow will do."

Norah smiled at him radiantly. Michael stopped talking suddenly and gazed at her, oblivious of everything, longing again ——

"What was I saying?" Then he went on quickly. "During the last month, in view of the condition of the Duke of Reichstadt, it has seemed necessary to tell the secret to the leaders of the great conspiracy. A *coup d'état* has been planned. Its accomplishment waits only for the death of the Duke at Vienna, which is a question of but a few days — we may hear at any hour. Our news will be in advance of all others. Then, at that moment, you will be brought forward, the only child of Napoleon, beyond any manner of doubt, and if our plans and our —"

He hesitated a moment, bit his upper lip sharply and rested his hand, as he stood before them, on a table close by. Then the frank, sincere face cleared, and with head high and a look of unselfish devotion shining from his eyes, he went on: " If our hopes come true — and it is hardly possible they will not — you will then be, by the grace of God, Empress of France."

Chapter Six

THE fire crackled — there was always a fire in the hall of Castle Kilmorra — and a heavy log fell in the dead silence. Then Norah lifted the strong young face that bore so striking a likeness now, in its gravity, to the great Corsican.

"Gentlemen," she said, "it is not a long story for so much. But it is a thing I must think over, and talk over with — my father, before I can give you an answer."

"An answer? *Une réponse?*" repeated the Marshal, looking be-

wildered. He did not understand.
But Talleyrand's smiling face became
suddenly grave and he said nothing.
His light eyes widened as if they
would take in Norah's very soul.

"It is no light matter to decide,"
said Norah.

"To decide?" echoed Marshal
Victor again, and then while all in
the hall waited for Norah's next
words to clear the uncertainty, with
power of English the old soldier
rushed into the breach.

"Her Highness responds us. Or
her Highness do not understand we,
or we does not understand her Gracious Highness's tongue. It is *nécessaire* to make part to her Highness
what is *nécessaire* — more clear. Talleyrand, *mon garçon* —" the great

diplomat started, then smiled —
" speak more clear the English then.
Why not ? I think well, it must be
to tell her Highness we have the
honor to place her on the throne of
La France "— the Marshal came nigh
to bursting in an effort to think up
the words of a fuller explanation, and
then ended in despair—" to-morrow
night."

Norah started and glanced at Michael, who looked as if he had been
struck.

" No, no," he said, " he cannot
mean that," and he turned to the
two with a rapid rush of French
interrogation, which was met by a
like earnest flood of answer from the
Marshal, with a smiling, quiet word
or two from the Prince. Michael's

face did not lighten, and Colonel
Fitzgerald's grew dark as he listened,
following more clearly at each word
the long unused language. Michael
turned to Norah.

" It is almost as bad." He caught
himself. " It is almost that," he
said. " You must be in Paris when
the news comes of the Duke's death.
They wish to leave here at the latest
to-morrow night."

" I will not," said Norah, calmly.

They all understood that and there
was consternation in the camp. " *Mon
Dieu! Mon Dieu!* " The Marshal
threw up his hands in horror.

" Norah alanna ! " remonstrated
Colonel Fitzgerald, looking up to
the face above him and dropping
into Irish in his excitement, " what

the devil are you meaning, my darling?" But Alex and Patrick and
Dennis came and stood behind the
two, tall and strong and formidable,
as if the guard had been called.

"And she sha'n't if she won't,"
growled Dennis, looking defiance
across the room at the Prince.

The Ambassador to England, plotting against his King with the easiest
conscience in the world, sat, smiling
as always, in a great arm-chair by
the fire. His head, its mass of thick,
silvery hair parted in the middle and
curling heavily in the neck, leaned
back, as if pleasantly weary, against
the dark carving. Folds of cobweb
linen, fresh and white, lay high around
his throat and against the soft, wrinkled cheek, and, below, a broad dark

velvet collar threw out the noble and
graceful head into sharp relief. One
leg was crossed easily over the other,
and the whole pose expressed a gentle
benevolence. Dennis's soul raged
within him as he met, helplessly, the
cheerfully amused look in the old
man's eyes.

"I will not have her Highness
scolded," said Talleyrand. "What,
am I to see all this army of great
men attack our sovereign lady, and no
champion to defend her but one lame
old man? *Eh bien,* so be it, then —
it is not the first time I have fought
against the world! And won! And
won, your Highness!" He turned
to her, and his eyes shone and his
voice was like a sweet trumpet-call.
He came limping across the floor

and put his hand on Norah's, who stood to receive him. "We will fight the world together — and we will win the battle, my lady. I — I have never failed, and you have never tried yet, but — " his eyes glowed as he looked at her — "you cannot fail!" In a moment he had them wrought up to enthusiasm and fervor — over what they had no time to think. Then, having dazed them so, he went on quietly: "The compact is made between us. Never fear, nothing can stand against us two," and he bent over again and kissed Norah's little hand. But the girl, of all in the room, alone kept her thoughts steady.

"Prince, I think you must be the most fascinating man in all the world," she said, smiling up at him, and Talleyrand smiled back, well satisfied. He believed it was so. He was glad to have her realize it.

"It is right," he said, "it is like your father — *mon Dieu!* but it is a clear touch of the Emperor — to see with your own eyes, to make your own plans — to refuse to hurry blindly. And yet, we must hurry you — I am desolated to think we must hurry you, my child. But it is imperative. There will be but one moment when we can put you on the throne — we must be there to seize it. As for the journey, the preparations — " he smiled kindly — "all that will be looked after for you. You go to a throne, my Princess, and ladies-in-waiting will surround you, to foresee your least need. All

that is my side of the compact,
and I promise you years of leisure
after this one forced march to your
capital."

"Monsieur," said Norah, looking
at him with eyes as self-possessed, as
gentle as his own, "you are very good
to me, but there is no compact between us yet. Not till I understand.
And it is not that I mind being hur-
ried — it is if I go at all."

The poor Marshal had another
nervous shock when he understood
this, which took a moment's effort.
Yet, astonished as were they all at
the difficulties thrown unexpectedly
in the path of glory by this reluctant
heiress to a throne, even the Marshal,
even the Prince was yet patient.

Talleyrand, glancing rapidly with

his eagle's eye over the whole situation, formed quickly his theory, but to the kindly soldier it seemed that a simple young girl recoiled from the unknown greatness thus suddenly thrust upon her, and needed encouragement.

So while the Prince planned the battle with scientific exactness, the Marshal, gallantly charging with the heavy artillery, fairly fell over himself to take up the wondrous tale.

"But see, your Highness, *ça m'étonne*. It is that *çe garçon-là, si bête*, he does not made you to comprehend. Ah, if it were I who had the youth and the English, so impossible. Ah! how then would I show you the picture of the beauti-

ful young girl to lead the armies of
France, who acclaim for her. *À
cheval* — how I say it ? On backing-
horse — in the costume — *en Ama-
zone* — in the habit — of — riding,
eh ? The regiments cry, speak, squeal,
shout — ah, yes, shout for the daughter
of Napoleon ! The old soldiers —
the soldiers *de l' Empereur* — it is they
who become mad of joy. It is what
the French love much, a picture, *un
effet*. It is the resemblance you have
at the great Emperor that is *merveil-
leuse*. Your eyes then, they burn like
the eyes of *le Grand Capitaine*. You
might *bercer* — rock, do I say it ? —
the nation, with the *petite main-là*.
It is to be the adored of La France,
your country to you ! A few days,
if you wish it, of the anxiety and

then — ah ! " Words failed the Marshal, English words at all events, and
he smiled ecstatically and closed his
eyes, while he thumped his breast
and raised open palms to heaven.

It seemed to Norah as if a friendly
thunder-storm were roaring about
her, to which the clear, quiet, incisive
voice of the Prince came as a relief,
with its claim, as before, of comrade-
ship, of protection. " *Eh bien*, then,
my little Princess, I shall not have
you bullied by these rough soldiers.
I think I see where you stand, clear-
headed young Bonaparte that you are.
You will not risk your great claim,
without knowing that the chances
are good — no, not even if old
Talleyrand-Périgord is risking with
you. You are wise and right —

though you do not know, perhaps, what they say of me, that so cautious an old fox I am, no prize is great enough to tempt me, if I burn even the tips of my claws. You see I have reputation for safety, at the least. Honor me now with your attention for a moment. I am a garrulous old fellow, but I will try not to be too long."

"You could not be, M. le Prince," said Norah, speaking as the Baroness had spoken in Paris, and looking at him with admiring eyes — women loved this man always.

"Your Highness is good to me." He flashed a smile at her. "I must tell you now as briefly as possible," and his words suddenly had the weight and gravity of a great statesman, "how my country and yours is situated. Not to mince matters, there is danger of anarchy. France, great France, is being made the private enterprise of a shopkeeper. Louis Philippe is King for Louis Philippe's benefit. The army, the public, the nation who have been treated as dry-goods, are in a most dangerous state of discontent. There will be a revolution, and if we, who have skill and patriotism and experience, do not steer well the ship of state, she will founder on the rocks. There is no other Napoleon to bring her safe through another storm. But there is one of his name, and with that name we, less great, but still old and wise, may yet conjure away the powers of evil, may yet save our dear land. Your Highness, you can have

no conception of the power of the
name you bear. To Frenchmen it
stands for France regenerated, for the
power to bring order out of chaos,
good government out of bad. That
is the general reason why our *coup
d'état* will be successful. For specific
reasons — I have lists of regiments,
of civil officials, of influential citizens, of arsenals — what will you?
— I have all these and more, in writing, with exactness. The Colonel
has seen them — I will show them
to you when you will. My comrade
that is, my Empress that will be —
I will not flatter you, but I will tell
you that with you on the throne, the
future of our country will be assured.
You have the Emperor's clear mind,
the Emperor's strong will, the Em-

peror's charm — you have your own
beauty and youth and sex that will
hold every gallant Frenchman as iron
holds a magnet. France demands
you. Reverence for your great father
must bring you. You bear your name
in trust for France. We will marry
you to a great Prince and a fortunate,
and the country will be secure.
Come then across the sea, and rule
over us, and France shall see bright
days, and I, and many another
white-haired subject of yours shall
die happy."

Back went the fine old head against
the high, dark chair, as if exhausted,
and Norah, looking at him with deep,
grave, thoughtful eyes, felt to the full
his fascination and his power. Hon-
ored beyond words she felt, because

she knew he was giving her his best
efforts. It was homage, not to an
Empress, but to a person ; not to her
birth, but to herself. There was a
long silence while all in the hall
watched the two strong spirits gazing
at each other, from the eyes of the
girl of twenty-one, and the man of
seventy-eight. Talleyrand was well
pleased. This was no cheap school-
girl personality, to forsake its position
at a touch. She must weigh his
words. She must sift the matter for
herself — that was reasonable, that
would prove he had not wasted his
powder, that she was indeed Napoleon's daughter. But of the end he
had no glimmer of doubt. He must
triumph, of course, he — the great
Talleyrand — over a girl — of course.

So he waited, smiling, satisfied. So long was the silence that Colonel Fitzgerald looked up at the girl against his arm to see what she was doing, alarmed a little for fear her mischievous spirit might not rise to the dignity of this occasion, and some mad prank might give them a wrong idea of his darling.

But he need not have feared. She lifted herself from the arm of his chair and stood by him, slipping her hand as she rose around his big one, which she held with a strong grip. Her great gray eyes swept the little circle calmly, all alike — her lover, her brothers, and the two great Frenchmen — and at once the power of her personality, that definite, indefinable quality, was felt.

"Gentlemen," she said, "it is now for me to make a little speech." Though she spoke to all of them, it was the Prince at whom she looked. "You speak of France as my country and say it demands me and my name — which I never knew was my name till just now. You say reverence for my father should make me go. Listen, then. It is not France that has been a country to me — it is Ireland, gentlemen. And it is Ireland that I love, not France. It is Ireland that I would shed my heart's blood for. And the Emperor may be my father — you say you can prove that to me. But what sort of a father is it that turns over his helpless child to strangers? — the kindest hearts of the world, to be sure, but that was

122

"The Emperor is nothing to me."

none of his doing. Why should I
give up home and life and all I love,
to do his pleasure, after I 'm grown
and worth the while, when he would
have none of me when I was small
and helpless? Here is my real father."
She bent and kissed the Colonel's
head. " The Emperor is nothing to
me. I care nothing for France."

The girl had been giving her lis-
teners a series of electrical shocks,
more unpleasant for being quite unexpected, but this topped them.
Even Fitzgerald groaned. " Ah!
Norah, my darling," he said, which
was severe to Norah, from the Colonel.
The Prince, from smiling confidence,
grew pale. He had made a great
effort. Could it be for nothing?
One could see that he was exhausted.

He looked about to faint as he lay back in his chair, and Alex poured quickly a glass of whiskey and water, so ill and worn was his face. It was Colonel Fitzgerald who cut short the nervous strain for them all.

"Norah, go to bed," he said. "Empress, or my little Norah, you need sleep. Gentlemen, you will get little good from further talk this evening. The night brings counsel, they tell me, and to-morrow morning we'll all be better able to give it and take it."

And within five minutes the Colonel, the last man up, was climbing the high, bare stairway, and Tim the butler was sleepily blowing out candles in the great darkening hall.

Chapter Seven

"MISS NORAH! Miss Norah!"
The name was called into
every room of Castle Kil-
morra next morning, and Tim the
butler and Kathleen, Norah's own
maid, and half the other servants put
their heads cautiously in, after excited
rapping, at door after door of the
big straggling place. But no Miss
Norah. Then Dennis, who was
second to none in guessing, ran
down to the stables, and when he
found Whirlwind gone, and Shamus
O'Shaughnessy not to be seen, and
Shamrock's stall empty besides, he

walked back to his father with a straight report.

"Norah's out on Whirlwind, with Shamus on the Shamrock."

The Prince smiled sarcastically, and looked just a touch bored.

The poor Marshal eyed Colonel Fitzgerald in despair. Were founders of a dynasty and saviours of their country ever before called on to chase a hoyden girl about the country, to put a crown on her head? Was it this way Irish gentlemen brought up their daughters? What might be the next move? Michael Ney came to the rescue.

"May I have a horse, Colonel?"

The Colonel, half apologetic, half chuckling, was regarding his visitors with the air of a benevolent mastiff who has caught a couple of birds of paradise and does n't know just what to do with them.

"Take the Saint and welcome, but it's little use, lad. No power can say what part of the country she's in by now. We'll just have to wait till her wild broth of a Highness chooses to come back again."

"I may happen to find her," said Michael. "I'll try my luck." And in ten minutes he was cantering down the avenue, with the sea shimmering through the trees at his left. For a while the road led along high cliffs ; and up against their base, and into the tiny harbors here and there, the broad Atlantic was rolling its deep blue tide. Absorbed though he was in one thought, he stopped his horse at the

point where his way turned from the
ocean, to look at the wonderful view.
Four hundred feet below him, in a
little bay, lay two or three fishing-
smacks, their sails flapping lazily
against the masts. He could see the
figures of the men as they passed
back and forth at work on the decks,
and their voices floated up to him soft-
ened by distance. Three miles beyond,
around the turn of the bay, spread the
group of little haggarts, or cottages,
that were Scattery village, gay in the
morning sunshine. But the eyes were
absent through which, for weeks, he
had looked at the loveliness of nature,
and he put his heel into the Saint,
swung sharply to the left, and galloped
on into the country like a man who
knows where he is going and the way

there. Four or five miles he rode
and then turned down a " boreen,"
or little lane, with tall, ragged hedges
on either side. Through the breaks
one could see that a ploughed field
lay on the right, but on the left a very
carpet of soft green turf. And now he
heard voices, and he caught his breath,
for one of them was the dearest on
earth. But the first distinct words
were in poor Shamus's rich Irish.

" Blessed Mary, Miss Norah, dear,
don't be goin' to make me take that.
'T is not for mesilf, but the poor
mither of me when I'm brought
back to her crippled for life an'
dead. Ochone! Plaze, Miss Norah."

" Shamus, I'm mortified at you.
Did n't I take it? Shame on you!
Over, then ! "

9   129

Michael heard a groan as of a man in extremity, then a rush down the turf, and he came out through a gap in the hedge just in time to see Shamrock and Shamus rise lightly over a five-foot wall, while Norah, holding Whirlwind back, watched critically.

"Be-eautiful! Beautiful, Shamus O'Shaughnessy," she cried. "You're really improving." Then as Michael rode up close beside her, she started a little at seeing him, but went on: "Isn't he improving? It's the highest bit of wall he's done yet." At this point Shamus, looking rather miserable, came up, after trotting around through the lane.

"Shamus, you're doing better. He's a terrible coward by nature, poor soul," she explained to Michael, "but I'm training him for it, and he's improving under treatment. Shamus, would n't you like to take the wall again, just to show Mr. Ney how brave you 're growing ? "

" No, plaze God, Miss Norah," said Shamus, shaking.

" Send him home," pleaded Michael ; " I want to talk to you."

" That's odd," said Norah. " It's the first time you ever did." But she turned to the groom : " Go home, Shamus O'Shaughnessy. You 're a good boy, but chicken-hearted. I shall not need you any more." And the lad, glad to escape from his adored but dreaded mistress, was off like a shot.

Before Shamrock's hoofs were through the gap in the hedge,

Michael's hand was on Norah's, and he was looking down at her eagerly, gladly, hopelessly — his eyes were full of a dozen meanings. For a moment there was one of those silences that are remembered like words, like events. Then Norah spoke, tremblingly.

" How did you know I was here ? "

" I knew," said Michael. " I think I could go straight to you if you were in the middle of China. I had to see you alone, and this chance came like a godsend. And now I must tell you — oh, how *can* I tell you ? " he groaned.

" What is it you want ? " asked Norah, simply, and smiled up at him with such a look — happy, proud,

shy, all in one — that he groaned
and bent over impetuously and kissed
her hand as if he could never tear his
lips away.

"What do I want? Only one
thing on earth. You, Norah. I
can think of nothing else. There's
nothing else I care for at all. If
you knew how wretchedly unhappy
I've been all night! To have found
you, to have won you even, and then
to give you up. O Norah, Norah!"
He put his face against her shoulder
like a child and held her hand tight
to his mouth. Norah trembled a
little, but sat still as a statue, looking
straight forward, holding Whirlwind
steady with little turns of her wrist.

"Do you mean — because of what
they said last night?"

"Yes — oh, yes."

"Only because of that?"

Michael straightened himself and looked at her, the hand still held against him.

"Only? Of course, only that — but, child, is n't that enough? You are as far out of my reach as the sun. They would never think of letting you marry me."

"Well then, sir." Whirlwind stirred at last, and the hand drew away and she faced around toward him defiantly. "I'll tell you this, though maybe you'll think me bold and forward. I — I — " The voice died down and her eyes fell before his burning ones.

"Tell me, Norah. Tell me quick. It's so hard to wait." He put his hand on her shoulder, and then she raised her eyes bravely and spoke fast :

"Do you think I'd let a little thing like that come between me and a great thing like — like — this?" She turned her head, and for a second her cheek lay on his hand.

It was a moment or two later that Michael said : "It's bitterly hard, but Norah, my Norah, I must give you up. I meant never to let you know this at all, that I — loved you. I should n't have loved you. I had no right."

"It would have been a poor sort of — love," said Norah, speaking the word softly, "that waited for leave to come."

"It is true," said Michael. "The

love waited for no leave. It came before I knew it, and I could n't have helped it if I had known. But I should n't have let you see it, Norah. The Prince and the Marshal trusted me. The leaders of the party in Paris trusted me. I was acting for France. It is necessary for my honor, as well as for my country, that I should give you up. Ah, if I had been strong enough not to let you see — if I had been the only one to be unhappy! It would have been far, far better. But now, poor child, you will suffer, too. Will you forgive me, Norah, for making you suffer? As soon as you are the Empress, dear, you will send me far away on some mission, and I shall serve you faithfully and love you always, but never come back to France until you have forgotten me, and I am strong enough to look at you calmly, and as I should look at my sovereign lady."

" Silly ! " said Norah.

Michael laughed delightedly, through his grief. It enchanted him to have her bully him. But his face filled with sadness again at once. "It must be so," he said, " dearest, dearest."

" Listen a bit," said Norah, " you who do so much talking. Is it true that if I were Empress, they 'd not let me — not let me — that I must marry someone of their choosing ? "

" I 'm afraid that 's inevitably so with people as great as you will be, Norah."

"It would interest me to see them choose a man for me," said Norah, her soft lips compressed; and Michael laughed again. "And suppose I tell them there's only one man I'll have?" She looked up at him a little embarrassed, a little pale. "I mean old Lord Kilkenny," she added, with a quick, mischievous smile, and then gravely again, "But if I said that, what could they do?"

"They could make it impossible, Norah, absolutely impossible. It is so now. In our wildest dreams we can't think of belonging to each other, dear."

"It means this, then. If I'm Empress of France, I can't — I can't belong to you?"

"No — my dearest."

"Up, Whirlwind!" And before Michael could speak again, his Princess was vanishing down the road at such a rate that he and the Saint had much trouble to keep her in sight, and could not begin to catch her till Whirlwind saw fit to shorten his stride and let the poor, white Saint within parleying distance of his dancing black feet and his tossing black head.

"Those papers," said Norah, turning in the saddle and pulling Whirlwind in short as Michael came up, "the papers they were to show me — they'll do that to-day?"

"I suppose so."

"Don't let them," she said, "I can't have it. I won't talk about it to-day. I must think. If they try

to make me talk, Whirlwind and I 'll
be off again, and you — " she flashed
a smile up at him — " even you
won't find us. To-night I 'll talk
to them, and I 'll tell them what
I 've decided."

" But, Norah, my darling," said
Michael, trembling but conscientious
yet, " it is to-night you must start for
Paris."

" Tell them, if I 'm going, I
will go to-night. And they 're to
have the papers to show me then."

" They are all here," said Michael.
" I will tell them. I will see that
they don't trouble you before to-
night. You shall not need to run
away again, Whirlwind." He put his
hand on the horse's neck and looked
down at the two, the spirited, alert,

brilliant animal, and the girl who sat
him, lightly, easily, perfectly, herself
a poem of spirit, alertness, animation.
It was there her beauty lay, more than
in line or color. It was a fresh, young
face, but uncommon only in the depth
and power of the look from her dark
gray eyes, and the charm, every moment changing, of her quick and
eager responsiveness. Michael looked
at her and was satisfied.

Chapter Eight

THE fire burned unobtrusively in the great hall of Castle Kilmorra. "To-night is not our time," the logs seemed to say to each other in a crackling, comfortable undertone. "To-night it is summer, and the soft air comes in from the window just by us; but we stay here always at our post, waiting for a word from the lord of the castle; and when the winds begin to howl about the Rock and the old walls, then, at his word, we leap into cheerful roars of red laughter, and go rushing up the chimney to defy the winter."

That seemed to be what the logs were saying, softly, steadily talking to each other. But nobody listened. Colonel Fitzgerald stood by the huge chimney, his tall sons standing near him, while, of his three guests, the Prince and the Marshal, the latter looking nervous and the former old and worn, sat near a table on which lay papers, and Michael Ney walked restlessly up and down, watching the door. No one tried to talk — all seemed absorbed in staring at the twilight sky and in listening to the waves that dashed up against the Rock — Castle Rock — a hundred feet below. It was a broad, high window, and below, as you looked down, you saw nothing but water, for this part of the old house of the

Fitzgeralds had been built two hundred years before, on the very edge of the great rock wall beneath it, that ran a quarter of a mile along the shore. From window to ocean was one sheer, plumb line. Only at the very base were a few ragged, big bowlders, and these the waves licked and dashed over so incessantly that they seemed but a part of the rough Atlantic Ocean, caught, petrified by the stone spirit of the castle some wild night long ago as they leaped in foam against the defiant walls.

Michael strode up and down; the Marshal drummed on the table; the Colonel gazed through the deep, open window. Talleyrand, throned in the large chair that had come to be called his, thought. His air was tranquil, disengaged. Yet his soul was not quite tranquil. His keen mind appreciated that, for all the apparent slightness of the obstacle to this affair that had seemed to them all so simple, their enterprise was in no small danger. He considered himself equal to it — oh, yes, he could yet control a girl, even Napoleon's daughter ! but the effort was more than he expected, and he was old and a little tired. As nearly as might be, with his even temper and his life of careful training, he was irritated. He had posted all the way from London twice within a month ; he had been at some pains to arrange the affairs of the embassy that nothing might suggest such a business as this before the time. He had exerted himself in several ways quite beyond his plans, and now, when his ship should be sailing in smooth waters and under balmy breezes, he found himself obliged to make further exertions. Carefully he considered the manner of them. On the whole, he concluded, it would be best to try sharpness, acidity, to cut into the steel of this young character so remarkably hard to influence. Sugar, it seemed, did not tempt her. One must then try wholesome medicine. He had seen wonders worked with a touch or two of his sarcastic tongue. But the trouble was, it must be done quickly. That boy at Schönbrunn, he might be dead now — the girl must be in Paris. Talleyrand would not see his plans fail for the vacillations of a child. Yes! He must

be decided, he must even be — alas!
— rough. So planned the old diplomat, with a look of gentle friendliness
on his face. No one spoke. The fire
gathered courage and snapped a loud
sentence or two in the silence.

The door opened and Norah came
in. At once the dead place was in
life. The old Prince rose a little
wearily and stood leaning on his cane,
watching the young girl intently, not
smiling as usual. Marshal Victor
sprung to his feet, soldierly, stiff;
Michael's restless step stopped short,
his broad shoulders looming high and
dark against the light as he faced
toward her, breathless. Norah walked
straight across the long room and
stood by him and next the table;
father and brothers, her old life, on

one side, the men who would put her
on a throne, the new, unknown life,
on the other. Between the two her
lover and herself.

There was a moment's grave stillness, and Norah placed her hand
on the table, on the papers that
were the only proofs of her strange
history.

" There is little to say," she began,
and her tones, though clear and even,
were low, " but it is hard to say it.
Gentlemen, I have to tell you that I
cannot go with you to-night. No,
nor later. My decision is quite made.
It would spare pain to us all could
you believe at once that I shall not
change."

Then the Marshal stood and thundered in his big voice that had the

note of tragedy heard in most French voices.

"It is not that it can be thus, this. The nation, La France, it demands you. The armies of La France for their leader, for the blood of the great Emperor, wait; it must that you come. Rise, rise to the so great time! I, I, your soldier, your general, I, your army, will protect you. There is not of danger. Child of Napoleon, advance! Seize your right! Fear not the danger! Look to the *gloire!* Have not of fear — I — I —" The English language ran dry.

Norah looked at him, her eyes burning dark. "You do not understand me, Marshal," she said, gently. "I am not afraid of anything." And

149

they all felt, looking at her with a thrill of admiration, that it was the bare truth.

"One sees, then, it is the spirit of her father, that which one hoped for, the same is the rock we split," groaned the Marshal.

"Mademoiselle, your Highness," said Talleyrand, from the great arm-chair, his head thrown back carelessly, his eyes, half-closed, gleaming at her. And at once every face, every eye was drawn toward that wonderful pres-ence. Stronger than ever before Norah felt the power of his magne-tism, though there was a new feeling of repulsion as she looked. She had never noticed before, she thought with astonishment, how bitter his mouth was, how cold and hard his

"Child of Napoleon, advance! Seize your right!"

eyes. But the voice that had a certain sparkling quality, most uncommon, though it carried to-night fire and hail, ice and snow, was as low and restrained as always. " It is not often that high heaven forgets its dignity so far," the Prince was saying, and Norah felt the old eyes burning hers, "as to put a nation's safety into the hands of a young girl, and when it does, I should think that even high heaven," with a sneer, " must see the error. At this time it happens by an accident of birth that you have the power to do an enormous amount of harm. It is only natural, I suppose, considering your age and your sex, that your first instinct should be to do that harm. It is most unfortunate that you should

151

happen to be of an importance quite
out of proportion to your personal
attributes, which are no doubt charming. It seems difficult to make you
understand that it is not your incli-
nations that concern us, interesting
as those may be. Whether or not
you care to be an Empress of France
is immaterial. You are, with all
respect, a figure-head — understand
that. I," he glanced at Victor, " I,
and others who know how, will rule
France. But the figure-head is absolutely necessary. We will have it —
you. Understand me, Mademoiselle.
We will have you. You may delay
us a day — two days, but the end will
be the same. You belong to us, and
we will have you. Appreciate at
once, and spare us further trouble,

that France and Talleyrand are stronger than you."

The Marshal had this day been marked by fate to be a bull in a china-shop.

" Have the courage, Mademoiselle, *votre Majesté*," shouted he in thunder tones, still convinced that all Norah needed was large quantities of encouragement. "Have the courage of your illustrious *père!* Show now the will of Napoleon at us! Let not obstacles de-de-deflect. But let one see now that the power of the will of the mighty Emperor is — is to you!"

Norah's clear, full tones fell like a sharp line of sunlight through a storm-cloud. " I will show it, M. le Maréchal — M. le Prince. If I have

153

the will of Napoleon, it is this way
I will show it, that I will not be
forced into doing what I choose not
to do. I will not give up my life
and my home and the man I love for
a country, a cause that is nothing to
me. I will not be an empress. I
care nothing at all for glory and ambition. My life is my own. I will
keep it — or give it to whom I
choose. I do not believe that I am
necessary to France. France will do
very well without Norah Fitzgerald.
I have decided."

Talleyrand, pale with exhaustion,
stirred to a deeper anger than he had,
perhaps, ever known before, but still
unable to believe his ears, to accept
defeat, still gallantly using his brain,
his force, his every power to arrest

this frightful landslide of failure, caught at one of the quick sentences that fell so rapidly upon each other.

" ' The man you love,' " he quoted, with a smile that was not sweet. " I might have guessed so much. *Cherchez l'homme* is true at times also, then. I gather the interesting news that there is then a man whom you love, Mademoiselle, better than an empire?" He asked it, for all his polished bearing and his smooth tones, with a scarcely concealed sneer.

Michael started with anger at the biting tone, but, standing close by her in the deepening twilight, he felt her sway a bit toward him and a touch of her shoulder against his. It was almost more than he could do to keep his arms from folding around

her when he heard her say, with
an effort, tremblingly, courageously,
" There is a man — whom I love
better — than an empire."

Then she seemed suddenly to feel
the packet of papers under her fingers.

" It is these that are the proofs of
my identity ? "

The Prince, his blood chilling,
thinking, planning fast, his philoso-
phy trembling in face of this madden-
ing threatening of defeat, paid little
attention to the question. " It is
these, Mademoiselle," he answered
curtly, not looking at her.

" Without these you would be
powerless to put me on the throne ? "
She asked it of the Marshal this
time.

" But yes, your Highness," the

Marshal said, seeing no object in this side issue, but concluding that the mysterious feminine mind, all-wonderful, all-difficult to follow, was approaching negotiations again from another point of the compass. " But yes, your Highness. Those papers there, so little, it is they that without what one could not make your Highness the Emper — Impératrice. It is impossible. It is that it is your throne you hold at the hand."

Norah turned, the eyes of all seven men following her with masculine deliberateness. The window-sill was low. In the stillness one could hear the waves dashing high, for the wind had risen, against the Rock. In a second she stood in the deep embrasure, and with one toss of her hand the priceless papers were flying far out through the air into the ocean.

The throne of Louis Philippe that had swayed in the balance was saved to the bourgeois monarch; a new line of sovereigns had ended before its beginning; a woman had dared to put aside the schemes, the plots, the feverish desires of hundreds of men, "with their triumphs and their glories and the rest," and with clear eye and steady hand had placed love above ambition and power.

Then she turned back again quietly and faced them, her head high, her look calm.

"The throne of France is no longer held in my hand or in yours," she said.

And as she stood in the breathless

silence, dark against the dark sky,
Michael's towering head close by
hers, the door opened at the farther
end of the great hall, and Tim the
butler brought in the lights.

www.ingramcontent.com/pod-product-compliance
Lightning Source LLC
Chambersburg PA
CDIIW050743230626
47155CB00005B/1894